To Heloise, for helping me hear the Silence. All my love
B.M.
To Em and my parents, who seek silence whenever I'm about
C.P.

THE SILENCE SEEKER
TAMARIND BOOKS 978 1848 53003 4

Published in Great Britain by Tamarind Books,
a division of Random House Children's Books
A Random House Group Company

This edition published 2009
1 3 5 7 9 10 8 6 4 2

Text copyright © Ben Morley, 2009
Illustrations copyright © Carl Pearce, 2009

Set in Baskerville

TAMARIND BOOKS
61–63 Uxbridge Road, London, W5 5SA

www.tamarindbooks.co.uk
www.kidsatrandomhouse.co.uk
www.rbooks.co.uk

Addresses for companies within The Random House Group Limited can be found at: www.randomhouse.co.uk/offices.htm

THE RANDOM HOUSE GROUP Limited Reg. No. 954009

A CIP catalogue record for this book is available from the British Library.

Printed and bound in China

The
SILENCE SEEKER

Ben Morley

Illustrated by Carl Pearce

Tamarind

Next door to Joe's house in the city a new boy and his family move in.

"He might come out to play!" says Joe.

"Yes," says Mum. "He might be tired though.

He has come from far away, looking for peace and quiet.

He's an asylum seeker."

"A Silence Seeker?" says Joe.

I have never met
a Silence Seeker before.
Every morning
he sits on the doorstep.
Sometimes he closes his eyes.
I think he's listening for a Silence.

I decided to help him.
I know all the quiet places
around here and,
if anybody can find
a Silence,
I can.
I made two jam sandwiches
and shouted to Mum that
I was off out.
The boy was sitting on
the doorstep as usual.

"Hello," I said.
"I'm Joe."
The boy just sat there.
"I live next door," I said.
"I know all the quiet places around here and
I can help you find a Silence...
if you like!"

The boy looked at me but
did not say a word.
I waved for him to follow and,
after a long while, he did.
He followed me like a shadow and
we went to all the quiet places
that I knew.

We went down to the laundry room
where the only noise is the click-clicking of the zips
hitting the washer windows.

But there was a group of biggies, banging and crashing and
jumping about to shouty music.

We went down by the canal
where the only noise is the drip-dripping
of water under the bridge.

But there was a gang of up-to-no-goods,
laughing and teasing and throwing stones.

We went down to the dump
where the only noise is the chink-chinking of glass
in the bottle banks.

But there was a bench full of down-and-outs,
mumbling and groaning and crying at the world.

When the street lamps buzzed on,
we went down under the flyover
where the only noise is the hum-humming of
cars overhead.

But there was a bunch of mischief-makers,
shouting and pushing and kicking cans.

It was getting late.
I knew Mum would be wondering
where I was and if I was all right.
So we went home.
On the way I gave the boy
a sandwich. He took it gently and
chewed it slowly.

The boy did not say a word
but he took my hand and smiled.
It was the first time he had smiled all day.
"Well, good night then," I said.
"I'm sorry we didn't find a Silence

               but we can keep looking tomorrow...
                    If you like!"

          The boy smiled again and
          went inside.

That night I lay awake
listening to the world.
It was noisy out there.

Early the next morning
I got dressed quickly and
took two slices of toast outside.
The boy was not on the doorstep.

I knocked
on the door.
No answer.
I rang the bell.
Nothing.

I had an idea.
I went down to the laundry room.
But the boy was not there.

I went down
by the canal.
But he was
nowhere
to be seen.

I went down to the dump.
He was not there, either.

I went down
below the flyover.
Nothing.
I went home.

I sat on the doorstep and
ate both pieces of toast.
My mum opened the door and
asked me what I was doing
sitting out there
looking so sad.

I told her I was looking for the boy and
she said that he had gone.
She said he left with his family
in the middle of the night
when I was asleep.
Then she told me to come indoors
before I caught a cold.

"Coming," I whispered.

Maybe it was too noisy for him here.
Maybe he has gone to look
for a Silence somewhere else.

I hope he finds it.

Before I went inside,
I closed my eyes and listened.

Just for a moment the city stopped
and took a breath and
everything was quiet...
but only for a moment.

OTHER TAMARIND TITLES
illustrated by Carl Pearce

For young readers aged 4 to 6 years

For older readers able to read alone

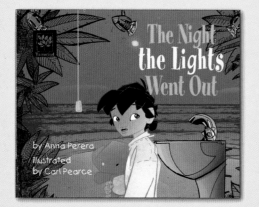

The Night the Lights Went Out
Anna Perera

The lights go out and Rana find herself alone in the dark… Dad comes upstairs to find her and take her down to the kitchen. But when the lights go on again Rana misses the warm, cosy darkness.

The rhythmical text confronts a child's fear of the dark and shows it to be unfounded.

Big Eyes, Scary Voice
Edel Wignell

Tania and Josh hear a scary voice calling in the park at sunset. They look and they listen and have an amazing twilight adventure. The park is full of strange shadows and things that look like eyes. The children, followed closely by Mum, wander through the falling light looking for the source of the scary voice…

Ferris Fleet and the Wheelchair Wizard
Annie Dalton

The Cosmic Peace Police, Mum's employers, need her to go on a mission. So Mum has to find a baby-sitter for Oscar, 8, and baby Ruby. They choose the cool, funky young magician, Ferris Fleet, and his magical wheelchair, Wonderwheels.
An exciting futuristic adventure story, featuring an enterprising little boy and his good friend, the magician in a wheelchair!

OTHER TAMARIND TITLES

FOR READERS OF *The Silence Seeker*

Amina and the Shell
Princess Katrina and the Hair Charmer
North American Animals
South African Animals
Caribbean Animals
The Feather
The Bush
Marty Monster
Starlight
Boots for a Bridesmaid
Yohance and the Dinosaurs

BOOKS FOR WHEN THEY GET A LITTLE OLDER...

TAMARIND READERS
Ferris Fleet and the Wheelchair Wizard
Hurricane
The Day Ravi Smiled
Reading Between the Lions

BLACK STARS
Rudolph Walker – Actor
Malorie Blackman – Author
Benjamin Zephaniah – Poet

The History of the Steel Band
The Life of Stephen Lawrence

BOOKS FOR YOUNGER READERS

Siddharth and Rinki
Danny's Adventure Bus
My Big Brother JJ
Big Eyes, Scary Voice
Choices, Choices...
What Will I Be?
All My Friends
A Safe Place
Dave and the Tooth Fairy
Time for Bed
Time to Get Up
Giant Hiccups
Are We There Yet?
Mum's Late

To see the rest of our list,
please visit our website:
www.tamarindbooks.co.uk